A Nose for Trouble

Don't miss any of the *paw*fectly fun
books in the **PET HOTEL** series!

#1: Calling All Pets!
#2: A Big Surprise
#3: A Nose for Trouble
#4: On with the Show!

PET HOTEL

A Nose for Trouble

by Kate Finch

illustrated by
John Steven Gurney

SCHOLASTIC INC.

Special thanks to Jane Clarke

For Helen and her guinea pigs, Ruby and Roxie.

No part of this work may be reproduced, stored in a retrieval system, or transmitted in any form or by any means, electronic, mechanical, photocopying, recording, or otherwise, without written permission of the publisher. For information regarding permission, write to Working Partners Limited, Stanley House, St. Chad's Place, London WC1X 9HH, United Kingdom.

ISBN 978-0-545-50183-5

12 11 10 9 8 7 6 5 4 3   13 14 15 16 17/0

Printed in the U.S.A.   40
First printing, October 2013

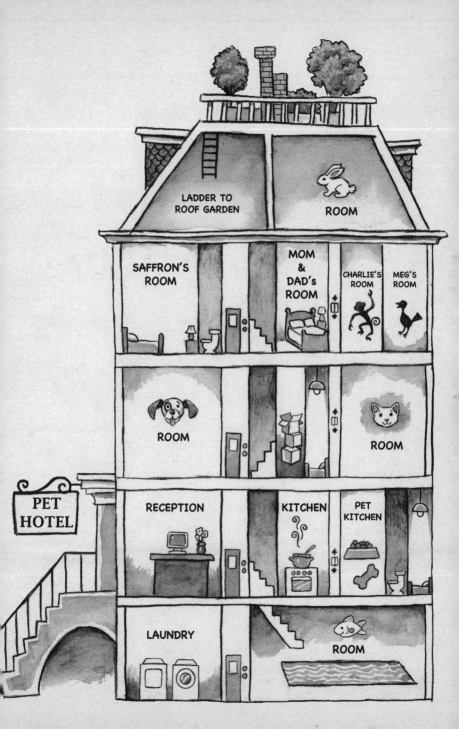

Charlie sat upright in bed with a start. His room was filled with a strange rumbling, whirring noise.

"What's that?" he exclaimed, turning on the light. The elephants, hippos, lions, and tigers on his wallpaper seemed to stare back at him.

Whirrr-zzz-zzz! The strange sound was coming from outside his room.

Could a guest at Pet Hotel be making all

that noise? The hotel was almost full of pet guests, for the first time since it opened. Charlie and his twin sister, Meg, had given their mom and dad the idea to turn Great-Great-Aunt Saffron's old hotel into a pet hotel, and now they were taking care of lots of cats and dogs and small furry pets. But as far as Charlie knew, none of them made this kind of noise. It sounded like a giant mechanical bee!

Charlie leaped out of bed and pulled on his paw-print bathrobe. He cautiously opened the door. Two shining lights, like eyes, were coming toward him down the hall.

Tingles ran up and down Charlie's spine . . . but it was only Meg, shining her pig-shaped flashlight at him. The two spots of light were coming out of its snout!

"What's making that noise?" Meg asked in a whisper.

"I don't know," Charlie murmured. "We'd better check on our guests."

They tiptoed down the stairs to the second floor, where the cats and dogs slept.

"The noise isn't as loud down here," Meg said softly as they peered into the Egyptian room, which had been turned into a special guest room for cats. The statues of pharaohs and the scratching posts in the shape of palm trees made spooky shadows outside the beam of the flashlight. Marmalade was licking her paws and washing behind her ears, and Oreo was stalking a toy mouse. Ginger, Mabel, Skittles, and Ollie were curled up, fast asleep.

"Cats are the best pets ever." Charlie sighed.

"You'll have your own soon," Meg whispered.

"Very soon!" Charlie grinned. Woody, one of the kittens who had recently been born at Pet Hotel, would be old enough to leave his mother and come back this week! Yesterday, Charlie had helped Mom and Dad set up a brand-new cat basket and litter tray for Woody in the corner of the kitchen. He'd spent all the allowance he'd been saving on kitty toys. Charlie couldn't wait for Woody to come and be his very own pet!

At the other end of the hallway, four of the five dogs staying in the forest room were also snoozing peacefully. Meg shone her flashlight around the dark room. The trees on the wallpaper made it look like a peaceful forest. Affie the Afghan hound and

Judy the Old English sheepdog were twitching as they ran in their sleep. Chico the Chihuahua and Amber the Lab were snoring loudly.

"Daisy's awake!" Meg pointed to the West Highland terrier, a frequent guest at Pet Hotel. She had her head tilted to one side as she listened carefully to the strange noise.

"Woof!" Daisy barked softly when she saw the twins.

"Shhhh!" Meg crept into the room and reached her hand into Daisy's pen to soothe her. She didn't want Daisy to wake up the rest of the dogs! If she started barking, that would wake Mom and Dad and Saffron — and Meg's own puppy, Buster, who slept in his basket downstairs in the kitchen. Daisy

licked Meg's hand and trotted back to her bed. Meg joined Charlie, who was creeping silently down the hall.

Zzz-zzz-whirrr . . .

It was hard to figure out where the noise was coming from!

Charlie stopped near the tiny dumb-waiter and put his ear to the hatch.

"It's definitely louder upstairs," he told Meg. "Let's check the guest room in the attic!"

"But there are only little furry animals up there," Meg said. "They're usually so quiet."

The twins tiptoed up the stairs. Charlie opened the door to the old playroom that had been painted to look like a meadow. It was bathed in silvery light from the full moon outside. The twins could see that, in the twelve hutches around the room, all the little animal guests were wide-awake! Many of the hutches had more than one pet inside, since most of the guests had arrived in groups of two or three. The five rabbits were hopping around, the eight gerbils were gnawing at their cereal bars, and the six guinea pigs made whistling noises as Meg and Charlie entered the room.

Whirrr-zzz-zzz . . .

"It's coming from that corner!" Charlie exclaimed, pointing.

They tiptoed across the playroom and stopped by the multistory hamster pen.

"It's Bluebell, Tulip, and Sweet Pea!" Meg gasped, pointing to the three dwarf hamsters who had arrived at the hotel earlier that day. They were running around and around on their exercise wheels, making them go so fast that their little feet were a blur.

Charlie and Meg grinned at each other. Pet Hotel's smallest guests were the ones making the biggest noise!

CHAPTER 2

The mechanical whir from the hamsters' wheels echoed around the room.

"Wheep!" whistled the guinea pigs.

"Eek!" squeaked the gerbils.

The rabbits thumped their back legs on the floor.

Meg groaned. "They'll wake up the whole hotel!"

"Maybe Dad can fix the wheels so they don't make so much noise," Charlie said.

Meg examined the wheels. They were fixed inside the hamsters' pen with red plastic clips. "We could just take out the wheels for now, and ask Dad in the morning," she suggested.

Charlie nodded. He grabbed an almost-empty seed tub. "We'll have to take Sweet Pea, Tulip, and Bluebell out first," he whispered, picking out a large sunflower seed. He carefully opened the top hatch of the pen and pressed his fingers against Sweet Pea's wheel so it stopped turning. Sweet Pea hopped off. Charlie held out the sunflower seed, and the tiny hamster's nose twitched.

"Aww!" Meg sighed. "The seed is bigger than her ears!"

Charlie scooped Sweet Pea out of the pen. The hamster's warm, pinkish-brown furry body was as light as a cotton ball in the palm of his hand. He gently stroked the dark brown stripe along her back and then placed her in the tub. Sweet Pea's shiny black eyes sparkled in the moonlight as she spotted the seeds left in the tub. She dropped the first sunflower seed and began to cram pine nuts into her cheeks.

"I love it when they do that," Meg said, giggling as she watched Sweet Pea's cheeks begin to bulge.

Charlie popped Tulip into the tub, next to Sweet Pea. The tiny yellow hamster's pink nose and white whiskers twitched in delight when she found herself surrounded by seeds.

"My turn." Meg reached into the hamster tank and stopped Bluebell's wheel. The teeny ball of blue-gray fur stepped into her open hand. Meg stroked the black stripe along Bluebell's back and gently pulled her out. But as she brought her toward the tub, Bluebell wriggled — and slipped through Meg's fingers!

"Oh, no!" Meg gasped as Bluebell skittered across the floor in the light of the moonbeams.

"She's heading for the doorway!" Charlie reached out his hand to grab the little hamster, but Bluebell dodged out of the

way. Thinking fast, Charlie whipped off his bathrobe and threw it across the doorway to block her path.

Bluebell hesitated for a moment, twitching her whiskers, then scurried toward the pile of fleece and burrowed into the soft folds of fabric.

Charlie picked up his bathrobe carefully

and found two tiny gray ears poking out of the front.

"She's hiding in my pocket!" Charlie carried his robe over to Meg so she could see.

"She likes it there — it's like a cozy hamster nest!" Meg smiled. Together, the twins gently transferred Bluebell to the tub with her sisters. Bluebell sat and groomed her ears for a second, then joined Sweet Pea and Tulip, stuffing seeds into her cheeks.

Meg and Charlie quickly unhooked the hamsters' wheels and pulled them out of the pen.

"Time to go back to bed," Charlie announced. Sweet Pea, Bluebell, and Tulip looked up from the tub. There wasn't a seed left, and the tiny hamsters' cheeks were so puffed out that their heads looked bigger than their round, furry bodies! Charlie tipped the tub gently into the bottom of the pen, and the three hamsters scurried out and disappeared into their nests of shredded paper.

"They'll be so busy taking the seeds out of their cheeks that they won't notice their wheels are missing," Charlie said, pulling his robe back on. His pocket felt warm where Bluebell had been snuggling.

"Phew!" Meg breathed a sigh of relief. "Now the other guests can settle down and get some sleep."

The twins closed the door of the old playroom behind them and crept downstairs. As they stepped onto the dark landing, a sudden rush of cool air ruffled their hair.

Flap, flap, flap!

Meg gasped. "What was that?" She shone the flashlight down the hallway.

Something was moving in the shadows behind the big potted plant next to the elevator.

"We don't have any birds staying with us." Charlie gulped. "Maybe it's a bat?"

They crept toward the shadowy creature, but before they could get a peek, it disappeared into the darkness.

"Turn off the flashlight — you'll scare it," Charlie whispered.

Meg clicked the switch, and the hallway plunged into darkness. Goose bumps ran up and down their arms as the twins edged forward. All of a sudden, Charlie yelled, "Owww!" and there was a loud *crash!*

"Woof!" barked the dog guests.

"Meoooooowww!" wailed the cats.

Meg's hands trembled as she clicked the flashlight back on. The plant, still in its big brass pot, was lying on the floor.

All along the hallway, doors were opening. Mom, Dad, and Saffron were awake. Oops!

"I knocked over the plant!" Charlie groaned as someone turned on the lights. "And we were trying so hard to be quiet!"

"Yip! Yip! Yip!" A fluffy golden puppy

raced up the stairs, wagging his tail. Buster had a brown marking around one eye that made him look like a pirate. Meg bent down to pet her puppy's furry ears. Buster licked her hand with his pink tongue.

"What happened?" Mom asked, tying the belt on her bathrobe.

"I bumped into the plant in the dark," Charlie said, picking up the toppled pot.

"What were you doing out of bed in the first place?" Dad asked, one eyebrow raised.

"The sound of the hamsters' wheels woke us up, so we took them out of the habitat. Then we heard something flapping down the hall," Meg explained, handing the hamsters' wheels to Dad.

"Flapping?" Saffron asked, wrapping a long red silk kimono around herself. Her hair hung down her back in two silver braids.

"But we don't have any bird guests. . . ." Mom sounded confused.

"That's what I said!" Charlie agreed.

"I'll check it out." Dad's robe swished as he marched down the hallway and back. "There's nothing here," he said reassuringly. "You must have heard the curtains flapping."

The barking and meowing faded, and Pet Hotel fell silent. Dad yawned.

"The guests have settled down, and we should, too," he told them as he headed back to bed. "Good night, everyone."

"Maybe you dreamed it," Mom suggested to the twins. She gave them both a hug, then trudged after Dad.

Meg and Charlie looked at Saffron.

"We *did* see something," Charlie told her. "A shadow . . ."

"I'm sure you did, my dears." Saffron's smile lit up her crinkled face. "Life is full of mysteries. But mysteries can be solved." She gave them a wink. "Be on the lookout for clues!"

CHAPTER 3

It was hard to get up the next morning in time to make breakfast for the hotel guests! Charlie and Meg yawned on their way downstairs. Dad was in the kitchen, working on the hamsters' wheels with his tool kit.

"I'm not sure I can make these any quieter," he told the twins as they headed for the old pantry that had been turned into a kitchen for preparing pet food.

Meg picked up a brown paper bag of Hamster Crunchies, which she and Charlie had bought from the Pet Bakery. They liked to give a few pieces to their hamster guests as a morning treat.

"There aren't any left!" she exclaimed.

"We bought them yesterday," Charlie said, wrinkling his forehead. "Bluebell, Tulip, and Sweet Pea can't have eaten *that* much!"

He peered into the bag.

"There's a hole in the bottom corner," he said. "Hmmm. Maybe it was nibbled by a mouse?"

Meg looked around. "There are no Crunchies or mouse droppings on the floor," she murmured.

"Aha!" Saffron's voice came from the doorway. "That bag could be your first clue in the case of the flapping shadow!"

Meg and Charlie suddenly felt wide-awake. They couldn't wait to solve the mystery, but first they had to serve the pets breakfast and take the dog guests out for exercise. They raced through breakfast in record time, then grabbed the dogs' leashes and loaded the dogs into the elevator. It creaked and clattered down to the hotel's main floor.

"You take Affie and Judy," Meg said, handing Charlie the leashes of the Afghan hound and the sheepdog. The big, friendly dogs peered at him through their shaggy fur and wagged their tails. "I'll take everyone else," Meg added.

She held Buster's and Amber's leashes in one hand and Chico's and Daisy's in the other as they stepped out into Gazebo Square. The sunny street was bustling with people shopping at the farmers' market, and the yummy smells of spices and coconut filled the air.

Daisy pulled back toward Pet Hotel as Buster tried to dash in the opposite direction, toward their friend Juan's booth at the market.

"I didn't forget to put your jacket on," Meg explained to Daisy. "It's just too warm to wear it today!"

Affie was dragging Charlie toward Chico, the little Chihuahua.

"He wants to walk next to Chico." Meg giggled. The Afghan towered over the Chihuahua. Chico was only as tall as his doggie friend's knee!

As the dogs pushed and pulled, their leashes were getting all tangled up.

"They're a real handful this morning!" Charlie said, trying to untangle himself.

"I have some special treats from the Pet Bakery in my pocket. Maybe I can use them to get these dogs to behave!" Meg pulled out the bag of treats. "Sit!" she commanded. Six eager, drooling faces watched as she put her hand into the bag.

"Good dogs!" Meg rewarded each of them with a small Doggie Cookie in the shape of a heart. Six tails wagged as the dogs got to their feet and headed for the park. Buster trotted slightly ahead.

"He's proud to be leading the pack!" Charlie laughed as Buster led them between the busy tents of the farmers' market, past a man selling posters, and under the archway into the park.

"Buster likes being the top dog at Pet Hotel," Meg agreed.

"When Woody arrives, we'll have a top cat plus a top dog," Charlie joked. "I can't wait!"

They stopped at Saffron's favorite bench, just inside the entrance to the park.

"Sit!" Meg ordered the dogs again. They all sat, panting and drooling.

"Good dogs!" Meg and Charlie fed them the rest of the heart-shaped treats. The dogs gobbled them up eagerly and licked their slobbery lips.

"Woof, woof, woof!"

Meg and Charlie looked up. On the path around the edge of the pond, a brown-and-white dog with floppy ears was tugging at his leash.

"Woooof!"

Then the dog tugged free of his owner and trotted across the park toward them!

CHAPTER 4

The dog stopped right in front of Charlie and Meg, panting and wagging his tail.

"He looks like a friendly little guy," Charlie said as the dog trotted slowly up to them, sniffing their hands and pockets with his shiny black nose. The dog's tan ears flopped over his white eyebrows. He had a dark brown and tan back, but his tummy, his muzzle, and the tip of his tail were white, and so were his legs from the knees down. He looked like he was wearing kneesocks!

"The Doggie Cookies are gone, but he can still smell them," Meg said with a giggle.

"He's a beagle," Charlie said. "I've read about them. They have an amazing sense of smell." He grinned as the beagle slowly wagged his tail, calmly greeting each of the dogs from Pet Hotel. Buster jumped playfully around him.

"Sit, Watson!" A woman wearing blue jeans and a light green shirt hurried up, pushing her curly red hair out of her eyes. Watson sat, and his owner took his leash.

Charlie and Meg looked at each other. There was something familiar about the woman . . . but what?

"I'm sorry about Watson," the beagle's owner told them as she pulled her hair back into a ponytail. "He's a retired police dog, so he likes to check things out."

"Officer McDonald!" Meg exclaimed.

"And you're Meg and Charlie from Pet Hotel, right?" The woman's freckly nose crinkled as she grinned.

The twins nodded. They'd often seen Officer McDonald patrolling the park, but they'd never spoken to her before.

"I know everyone who lives around Gazebo Square," Officer McDonald explained, "but very few people recognize me when I'm not in uniform. You two are very observant — just like Watson."

She pointed to the beagle, who was snuffling around the park bench. "Watson used to work at airports, sniffing out suspicious baggage. I adopted him when he retired last month. He has an amazing nose for picking up scents. Just tell him 'Seek,' and he can sniff out almost anything."

"I noticed! He could smell our doggie treats from across the park!" Meg agreed.

Watson's nose looked like it was glued to the ground as he sniffed along.

"He thinks he's still in the police, looking for clues," Charlie joked.

Just then, Officer McDonald's cell phone rang.

"Excuse me for a minute." She turned away to take the call. When it was over, she walked back to the twins, looking worried.

"I have to report for duty and interview some witnesses at the local hospital," she said. "Only police dogs are allowed in there, and Watson isn't a police dog anymore. So now I need someone to take care of Watson for the rest of the day."

Meg glanced at Charlie.

"We have space left for one more dog," Meg told her.

Charlie nodded. "Watson can be our very first day-guest at Pet Hotel!"

CHAPTER 5

"Thank you so much. I'll come by to pick him up later!" Officer McDonald handed Watson's leash to Meg with a bright smile and rushed off.

Meg and Charlie led the dogs under the archway and out of the park. Watson's nose was still low to the ground. Meg laughed as she noticed that Buster, who was trotting along beside Watson, began to copy him.

She nudged Charlie.

Watson was sniffing along slowly and methodically, holding his white-tipped tail stiffly in the air. Buster, on the other hand, was snorting and sneezing, and his furry golden tail was wagging so fast that it was a blur.

"You can tell Watson's a professional sniffer," Charlie joked as Watson delicately sniffed at a box of cardboard tubes set up next to a display of posters on sale near the park railings.

Buster bounded over to join Watson. He accidentally bumped into the box and sent the tubes rolling all over the ground.

"But Buster has a lot to learn!" Meg groaned. "Sorry!" she called to the poster seller. "He's only a puppy. I'll pick them up!"

She put the dogs' leashes into Charlie's hands.

"Sit!" Charlie ordered, feeling a little nervous. He'd never been in charge of seven dogs before. What if one of them saw a cat?

To his relief, the dogs sat obediently as Meg began to gather up the sturdy cardboard tubes.

"I like dogs," the poster seller said with a smile, holding out the box. "It must be fun to have so many!"

"Only Buster belongs to us," Meg told him as she carefully packed the tubes back into the box. They were like giant versions of the cardboard tubes you'd find in the middle of a roll of paper towels. "The others are our guests at Pet Hotel."

"That explains it." The man chuckled. "Don't worry about the tubes. They're empty, and I don't need them anymore — I'm just saving them for recycling."

As Meg looked at the tubes, an idea occurred to her. "They'd make great tunnels for hamsters!" she exclaimed.

"PERFECT!" Charlie agreed. "We can make a hamster playground inside their habitat — then they won't miss their squeaky wheels!"

"That's one way to recycle tubes that I'd never thought of," the poster seller said with a laugh. "You're welcome to take as many as you like."

"Thanks!" Meg filled her arms with tubes.

Suddenly, from behind her, there was a deep *"Woof!"*

Watson was sitting, as he had been ordered to, but he was pawing at a small piece of paper on the ground.

"What did you find?" Charlie asked. Watson stood up and sniffed so hard at the paper that it stuck to his nose! Charlie peeled it off and unrolled it. The piece of paper was the size of a candy wrapper. There was a message written across two fold marks:

Come over for some apple pie!

"It looks like a spy message!" Charlie said with a gasp. "Maybe 'apple pie' is code for something, like a secret package. It's been rolled up to fit in a tiny place. But where did it come from?"

He handed it to Meg.

"Another mystery!" Meg said. "But now we have an expert clue sniffer to help us out. Seek, Watson!" She held the paper to the beagle's nose.

Watson sniffed deeply.

"Ahrooo-woo-woo!" he howled.

"He sounds like a foghorn!" Meg giggled as Watson lowered his head to the ground, tugging at the leash. Buster, Affie, Chico, Judy, Amber, and Daisy followed his lead. The dogs raced off, dragging Charlie along behind them. Meg ran after them, clutching the cardboard tubes to her chest.

They skidded to a stop at the fountain next to the gazebo.

Meg and Charlie peered around, then looked at each other in confusion. There weren't any spies, just a pigeon fluttering its feathers and ducking its head in the fountain as it took a bath. . . .

"Woof!" Watson barked.

The pigeon froze.

"Look!" Charlie whispered, pointing to the pigeon's leg. There was a tiny metal tube strapped to it.

"The message must have fallen out of that container!" Meg guessed.

But before they could get any closer, the pigeon took off in a shower of sparkly water droplets. The bird soared over the twins' heads and flew across Gazebo Square, out of sight.

CHAPTER 6

The bells on Saffron's earrings jingled as she opened the door of Pet Hotel. The twins couldn't help smiling when they saw her. She was wearing an eye-popping outfit patterned with neon pink and orange flowers.

In a flurry of excitement, Meg told her about Watson, and Charlie told her about the pigeon.

"I think you saw a carrier pigeon," Saffron declared, throwing a white-and-purple feather boa around her neck. "They're trained to deliver messages."

"Like old-fashioned pigeon post?" Meg asked as she set the tubes down on the reception desk. "Cool!"

"But who sent the message?" Charlie wondered, still holding on to the dog leashes.

"That's a mystery," Saffron said with a wink. "For now, how about I take Buster into the kitchen while you settle our doggie guests?" She trailed her feather boa along the floor in front of Buster's nose. He bounded after it, his tail wagging wildly as he tried to pounce.

"Buster really does LOVE playing with Saffron's boas," Meg said with a laugh.

"I think it's a great idea to replace the hamsters' wheels with tubes," Dad agreed when the twins explained their new plan.

It was fun cutting up the poster tubes and putting them together to make tunnels and hiding places. After about an hour of building, Meg and Charlie proudly carried the finished hamster tubes up to the old playroom. Sweet Pea, Tulip, and Bluebell

stayed in their nests as the twins fitted the tubes into the hamsters' habitat.

"Playtime!" Meg whispered. The twins both held their breath as three tiny noses poked out of the nests, whiskers quivering. Bluebell hesitantly stuck her head into the end of one of the tubes. Her furry body disappeared, closely followed by Sweet Pea's and Tulip's. Soon, the three dwarf hamsters were scampering happily in and out of the tubes. Except for a quiet rustling noise, they barely made a sound.

"Awesome!" Charlie exclaimed. "They're having a great time, and now the other guests will get some sleep tonight."

"So will we!" Meg agreed happily. She filled the hamsters' water bottles and added the last of the special hamster food to their bowls, but Bluebell, Tulip, and Sweet Pea were so busy playing in the tubes that they didn't even stop to nibble.

"We'll need to buy some more Hamster Crunchies at the Pet Bakery tomorrow," Meg told Charlie.

"We still don't know who got into the bag in the kitchen," Charlie pointed out.

"Or what was flapping down the hallway last night," Meg said thoughtfully. "Hey!" she exclaimed. "Watson's good at following clues. Why don't we see if he can solve the mystery of the missing Hamster Crunchies?"

"And the mystery of the flapping night visitor!" Charlie jumped to his feet, grabbing the empty bag of hamster food.

They sped to the forest room, and Meg clipped on Watson's leash. Charlie held the empty hamster food bag under the beagle's nose.

"Seek!" he told him.

Watson sniffed deeply. Then his tail stiffened. *"AHROOO-WOO-WOO!"* he bayed, putting his nose to the ground and zooming off with his ears flapping. The twins tore after him.

Watson was on the case!

CHAPTER 7

Watson stood on the third-floor landing with his nose in the air. He headed for the potted plant that Charlie had knocked over the night before.

"He's picking up the scent trail!" Charlie remarked.

"Snurrrffff!" The beagle sniffed noisily.

Meg bent down and picked up a seed from the carpet.

"It's a Hamster Crunchie!" she said.

"It's a clue," Charlie corrected her. "Watson's on the right track!"

With that, the beagle put his nose to the ground again. Slowly and deliberately, he padded toward Saffron's bedroom. He stood in front of the closed door and gave a low, soft howl: *"Woo-woo-ahroo!"*

"I'll ask Saffron if we can go inside." Meg shot downstairs and came back with a grin

on her face. "Saffron says, 'My door is always open to you, my dears, even when it's closed.'"

Charlie couldn't help laughing. "I guess that means we can go in," he said, pushing open the door.

Saffron's room was like a fancy, colorful tent. The ceiling was draped with turquoise and pink silk that spilled down over the swirly wallpaper. Watson sniffed around Saffron's bed. He stuck his nose under the yellow, blue, and purple patchwork quilt that hung down to the floor. The white tip of his tail twitched excitedly.

"He found something!" Meg reached under the bed and pulled out a wicker basket. Watson scuttled out backward and sniffed eagerly at it.

"It's Saffron's collection of feather boas."
Meg held up a thin, bright green feather
boa in one hand and a thick purple one
in the other. Saffron's turquoise boa was in
the box, too, along with some boas that Meg
had never seen before. Meg draped them
around her neck as she checked them out
one by one. As she pulled out an orange
boa, Watson gave a deep *"WOOF!"*

Charlie examined it closely. In the midst

of all the orange ostrich feathers, there was a dark gray one.

"Another clue!" Charlie exclaimed, holding it up. "It's from a bird . . . but most birds don't fly at night."

"But it was bright last night, because of the full moon!" Meg said excitedly. "Birds like seeds. So a bird would like Hamster Crunchies . . ."

". . . and a bird's beak could easily poke a hole in a bag of hamster food," Charlie agreed. "But how did it get in? Saffron always keeps her door shut."

"It must have flown into her room when she came out into the hallway with Mom and Dad, after you knocked over the plant," Meg said thoughtfully, stuffing the boas back into the wicker basket.

"Then it nested in the boa basket until morning," Charlie deduced. "So it definitely wasn't a bat we saw, it was a bird!" He held the gray feather under Watson's nose. "This is who we're looking for," he told the eager beagle.

Watson's tail shot up as he trotted down the hallway. The twins followed him upstairs. He led them to the bottom of the little iron ladder on the top floor, which led up to the roof garden.

Watson pointed his face to the ceiling. *"AHROOO!"*

Meg and Charlie looked up.

"The hatch isn't closed the right way!" Charlie cried. "There's a gap big enough for a bird to fly through."

Meg scrambled up the ladder and pushed open the hatch.

There was a flutter of wings as a big pigeon flew off and perched on the railing around the pretty roof garden.

Meg clambered onto the roof, closely followed by her brother. She pointed silently at the pigeon. They'd seen Saffron feeding

pigeons up here, but never one as beautiful as this. It had clean pink feet, a light gray body with dark gray wings, and shimmery purple and green neck feathers.

"It has a metal tube strapped to its leg!" Charlie gasped. "That's our carrier pigeon — and it must be the thing that flapped by us last night."

The pigeon flew off before the twins could do anything else.

"It must have come into the hotel to look for food," Meg said. "I'll bet Hamster Crunchies are a nice change from birdseed."

Charlie rummaged in the pocket of his jeans and pulled out the note they'd found outside the park.

"Now we just need to figure out

who that pigeon belongs to," Charlie murmured. "Then we can crack the apple-pie code."

"That will take some more detective work." Meg grinned as she peered down through the open hatch. Watson looked eagerly back up at her. "Watson looks ready to go!"

CHAPTER 8

"We should check out the fountain," Charlie said as they headed back to Gazebo Square with Watson. "That's our best chance of finding the pigeon."

It was hard to wait patiently once they arrived at the fountain, but finally the pigeon fluttered down to take a drink. Charlie, Meg, and Watson watched as it took off again.

"There!" Meg pointed down a narrow

side street lined with trees. The pigeon was sitting on a branch. It was a quiet and peaceful little street. The brownstones were set back behind identical iron gates.

"That looks like just the place for a spy to live," Charlie remarked as the pigeon flew down and briefly settled on a gatepost farther down the street. Then it took off and swooped over the row of houses.

"Which gatepost was it sitting on?" Meg asked with a groan. "It moved before I could check!"

Watson raised his muzzle and sniffed the air. *"Ahroo!"* he announced, stopping in front of one of the gates.

Behind it was a narrow front yard full of apple trees covered with ripe red fruit. On the path just inside the gate was a box of apples. A sign nearby read:

FREE APPLES

HELP YOURSELF!

"Wooof!" Watson barked.

The twins looked at each other.

"Maybe the note isn't written in code after all," Meg said. "Maybe it really *does* mean 'Come over for some apple pie!'"

Charlie led the way up the path. "There's only one way to find out."

"*Snurfff!*" Watson waddled up the path, sniffing loudly.

"Watson's still sniffing out clues. This must be the right place!" Meg said confidently as they reached the front door of the house. She pressed the doorbell.

A girl with a cloud of dark hair answered the door. She looked a few years older than the twins. "Hi there. Can I help you?"

"Hi! We're Meg and Charlie, and this is Watson," Meg replied. "We're from Pet Hotel, around the corner."

The girl grinned. "Sure," she said. "I've seen you two walking huge packs of dogs in the park! Looks like fun."

"It is," Charlie said with a smile. "Hey, this might be a strange question, but do you keep carrier pigeons? One got inside our hotel the other night."

The girl's eyes widened. "Yes, I do!" she said. "It's my hobby. But I didn't realize they were breaking into other buildings! I'm so sorry."

Meg shook her head. "Don't worry. It flew into our open roof hatch, and all it did was eat some hamster food and leave a feather behind," she said reassuringly. "We just wanted to solve the mystery."

"We found a note." Charlie dug into his pocket and held it out. "I thought it might be in code."

The girl looked at it and giggled.

"Come inside and see," she said. "My name's Polly, by the way."

Watson sat at attention by the front door as Meg and Charlie went inside. Polly led them out onto an upstairs balcony. It was as wide as the house, and at the end was a domed wooden hut with lots of small arched windows. The pigeon they'd been tracking was sitting on top of it! Inside the hut, other pigeons cooed contentedly.

Polly reached for the beautiful bird.

"Meet Biggles," she announced, scratching the back of the carrier pigeon's neck.

"Hi, Biggles!" Meg greeted the bird as she and Charlie gently touched its soft, shimmery neck feathers.

"Ooo-ooo," Biggles cooed.

"When he came back with an empty container, I thought the note had been delivered," Polly told them.

"Who was the note for?" Charlie asked.

"My grandfather," Polly explained. "Gramps has loved pigeons since he was a boy — that's how I got interested in keeping them as pets. It's fun to send each other messages by pigeon post!"

"So your note wasn't in code after all." Charlie chuckled.

"But now your grandfather won't know that you invited him to come over," Meg said.

"That's okay," said Polly. "I can ask Gramps another time. Since you're here, would you like to help me feed the pigeons? Then we can each have a slice of freshly baked apple pie!"

⋈ ⋈ ⋈

Later that day, Pet Hotel's doorbell rang.

"That should be Officer McDonald, coming to get Watson," Mom called. Charlie and Meg rushed to clip on Watson's leash. Buster stood beside them, wagging his tail as they opened the door.

"Hello again!" Officer McDonald bent down to pet Watson's ears. Standing on the doorstep next to her was Carmen from the cupcake stall at the farmers' market. Carmen held a cat carrier. Her face broke into a smile when she saw Charlie.

"Guess who this is!" she said.

Charlie couldn't help jumping for joy. "Woody!" he yelped, peering through the wire door at the front of the carrier. The little black-and-white kitten pressed his head against the wires.

"I don't like good-byes, so I'll be back later to say hello after he's all settled in!" Carmen handed Charlie the cat carrier, blew Woody a kiss, and left with a wave.

Meg, Watson, and Officer McDonald watched as Charlie gently scratched the top of Woody's soft head through the door.

"Yip, yip, yip!" Buster bounded up, yapping excitedly. Watson sniffed the air.

"Buster, meet Woody!" Charlie carefully lowered the cat carrier to dog-nose level. "He's going to live at Pet Hotel, too."

Buster's ears drooped, and he backed away.

"I hope he's not going to be jealous!" Meg whispered.

Watson snuffled curiously at the carrier. Buster watched with his head tilted to one side as Watson wagged his tail and calmly greeted Woody. Then the fluffy golden puppy playfully bounded forward, sniffed curiously at Woody's carrier — and wagged his tail, too!

"Buster, you're a copycat dog!" Meg giggled, stroking his furry back.

"Time to go." Officer McDonald and Watson turned to leave. "Thanks for taking such good care of Watson, kids. See you around!"

"You're welcome," Meg and Charlie called after her. "Good-bye!" They stepped back into Pet Hotel and closed the door.

Charlie and Meg kneeled beside the kitty carrier in the kitchen. Buster sat next to them, wagging his tail from side to side on the tiled floor. Saffron watched from her comfy chair in the corner.

Charlie opened the front of the carrier and took Woody into his arms. He finally had his very own kitten! He gently tickled Woody under the chin. Woody purred and purred.

"Welcome, Woody," Saffron murmured. "You're part of the family now!"

The twins beamed at each other. They could hardly believe it. A kitten for Charlie and a puppy for Meg. It was like a dream come true!

PET HOTEL

Check out who's checking in — don't miss the next Pet Hotel book!

Pet Hotel #4: On with the Show!

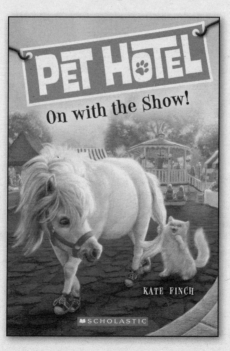

CHAPTER 1

"It's here, it's here!" Charlie yelled, throwing open the front door of Pet Hotel. Parked right outside was a very long, shiny black car. The driver stepped out and held open the door. She was wearing a gray suit, a sleek hat, and large sunglasses.

"We get to ride in that?" asked Meg, Charlie's twin sister. "Amazing!"

"Wait for me," their Great-Great-Aunt Saffron called as she followed the twins down to the sidewalk. The driver took Saffron's arm and helped her into the car. Little mirrors sewn into her long sunshine-yellow dress flashed, and the bells on her earrings jingled as she settled herself into the white leather seat. Meg and Charlie sat on either side of Saffron and buckled their seat belts. They were wearing their best jeans and matching new T-shirts that read Pet Hotel above a cute drawing of Buster, who was Meg's puppy, and Woody, who was Charlie's kitten.

"I feel like a movie star!" Saffron murmured, patting her silver hair and throwing a purple feather boa around her wrinkly neck.

The twins giggled. They were bursting with excitement. A movie star's pet was coming to stay at Pet Hotel — and the limo was taking them to collect their new guest.

Meg and Charlie gazed out of the tinted windows as they drove past Gazebo Square. The huge car had to move slowly because the market was packed with people bustling around brightly colored food stalls.

Charlie lowered the window when they reached their friend Juan's Cocina Mexicana stand. The delicious scent of limes and chillies wafted into the car. Juan was standing underneath the stall's green-and-white striped canopy.

"Hey, Juan!" Charlie called. "Look at us! We're in a limo!"

When Juan spotted them, his mouth dropped open.

"*Hola*, my friends!" he called with a chuckle, bending to pick up his puppy, Paco.

Charlie and Meg leaned out of the windows, grinning and waving as the limo turned onto Park Street. Juan held up Paco's paw and wiggled it, so it looked like he was waving back.

The driver threaded her way through the busy city and finally pulled up to a tall apartment building that backed onto a tree-lined park.

"This is very fancy!" Saffron exclaimed, pointing to the golden canopy over the entrance. A doorman in a dark suit and cap hurried to help them exit the limo.

"Miss Penigree is expecting you," the doorman said, as he ushered them through the glass door into a marble-lined hall.

"Take the elevator to the penthouse apartment on the thirty-third floor."

He pressed the elevator button and stood back so the twins and Saffron could step inside. The doors closed and they were whisked up to the penthouse.

"This is a zillion times faster than our clunky old elevator at Pet Hotel," Meg said.

"Miss Penigree must be very rich to live here," Charlie declared.

"My dears, Miss Penigree was a huge star in the 1960s," Saffron explained. "She was in *Moonlight Mystery, Romance on the River*, and *Follow the Sun*." Saffron sighed. "I loved her in that. So wild and carefree! I hope she hasn't changed."

The elevator doors slid open to reveal the penthouse apartment. A butler wearing an old-fashioned black bow tie and white gloves was waiting for them. He looked down his nose at Meg and Charlie's jeans and T-shirts.

"You must be here to pick up Velvet, Miss Penigree's pet," he said.

Meg, Charlie, and Saffron exchanged disappointed glances. Maybe they weren't going to meet Miss Penigree after all.

But then a loud, clear voice rang out above them.

"One moment!" An elderly woman wearing a cream silk dressing gown swept down the grand marble staircase next to the elevator. Her frosty silver hair was piled neatly on top of her head and fixed with sparkling diamond pins.

"Miss Penigree!" Saffron breathed.

The movie star regarded them sternly.

"I need to make a few rules clear," she announced. "Velvet is a pedigree Persian show cat and must be kept spotlessly clean. I must insist that you always, always, ALWAYS wash your hands before touching Velvet. My cat is a perfect example of the breed and MUST be ready for the Celebrity Pet Show when I return from the awards ceremony in Los Angeles!"

Meg and Charlie exchanged a nervous glance. Would they be able to take care of a movie star's pet?

Miss Penigree led the twins and Saffron inside her penthouse apartment. Meg gasped at the huge oil paintings on the walls and Charlie gazed up at the chandelier glittering near the ceiling.

"It's time you met Velvet," Miss Penigree said. "But first, as I said . . ." She clapped her hands and indicated the bathroom. They trooped in one after the other.

"I like the gold statue by the sink,"

Charlie told Miss Penigree when he came out again.

"Statue? That's not a statue," Miss Penigree informed him. "That's an Oscar!"

"It's the top award for acting," Saffron explained. "Miss Penigree won it for *Follow the Sun*. I loved you in that," she told the movie star.

"Thank you. It was my finest hour." Miss Penigree sighed. "Now, please show me your hands."

Charlie, Meg, and Saffron reluctantly held out their palms for inspection. Miss Penigree examined their hands carefully and nodded approvingly.

"Follow me to Velvet's bedroom." Miss Penigree strode off along a red carpeted hallway lined with black-and-white photos.

"There she is in *Romance on the River*," Saffron whispered, pointing out a picture of a young Miss Penigree wearing a safari hat. Another photo showed a glamorous middle-aged woman in a sequined evening gown. "That's Miss Penigree accepting her Oscar," Aunt Saffron explained.

Miss Penigree carefully opened a door. The twins blinked. Everything in the room was white, including a cat-sized four-poster bed, with heart-shaped pillows and a quilted comforter. On top of the bed a large white cat with long downy fur was curled up, fast asleep.

WHERE EVERY PUPPY FINDS A HOME

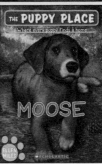

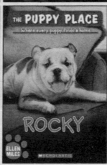

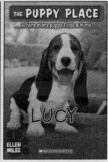

KITTY CORNER

Where kitties get the love they need

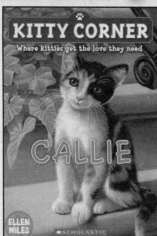

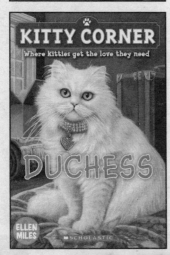

These purr-fect kittens need a home

SCHOLASTIC